Dear Parent:
Your child's love of reading starts here!

Every child learns to read in a different way and at his or her own speed. Some go back and forth between reading levels and read favorite books again and again. Others read through each level in order. You can help your young reader improve and become more confident by encouraging his or her own interests and abilities. From books your child reads with you to the first books he or she reads alone, there are I Can Read Books for every stage of reading:

SHARED READING
Basic language, word repetition, and whimsical illustrations, ideal for sharing with your emergent reader

BEGINNING READING
Short sentences, familiar words, and simple concepts for children eager to read on their own

READING WITH HELP
Engaging stories, longer sentences, and language play for developing readers

READING ALONE
Complex plots, challenging vocabulary, and high-interest topics for the independent reader

ADVANCED READING
Short paragraphs, chapters, and exciting themes for the perfect bridge to chapter books

I Can Read Books have introduced children to the joy of reading since 1957. Featuring award-winning authors and illustrators and a fabulous cast of beloved characters, I Can Read Books set the standard for beginning readers.

A lifetime of discovery begins with the magical words "I Can Read!"

Visit www.icanread.com for information
on enriching your child's reading experience.

Monsters vs. Aliens: Ginormica's Big Battle
Monsters vs. Aliens ™ & © 2009 DreamWorks Animation L.L.C.

Library of Congress Catalog card number is available.
ISBN 978-0-06-156726-1

Typography by Rick Farley

❖

First Edition

09 10 11 12 13 LP/WOR 10 9 8 7 6 5 4 3 2

I Can Read!

READING 2 WITH HELP

DREAMWORKS

MONSTERS VS ALIENS

GINORMICA'S BIG BATTLE

Adapted by Gail Herman
Pencils by Charles Grosvenor
Color by Artful Doodlers

HarperCollinsPublishers

Susan Murphy was an ordinary person planning an ordinary wedding.

She wanted to live an ordinary life.

Then one day, a meteor struck.

Boom!

The meteor knocked Susan down.

When she got up, she was a giant.

She was a monster.

She was Ginormica!

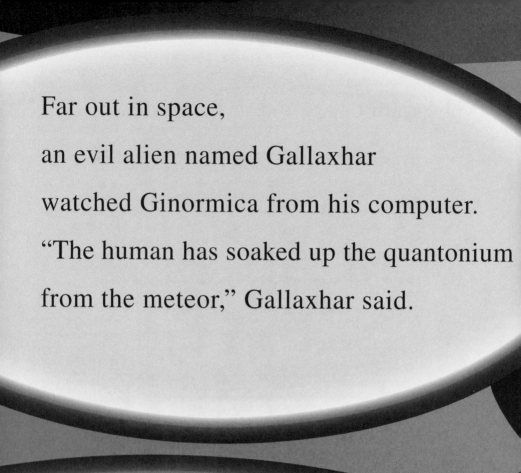

Far out in space,
an evil alien named Gallaxhar
watched Ginormica from his computer.
"The human has soaked up the quantonium
from the meteor," Gallaxhar said.

"It's made Ginormica big and strong.

But the quantonium is mine!"

Gallaxhar said.

"I must have it to rule the world.

Get her!" he ordered his robot.

The robot raced to Earth.
When Ginormica saw the robot,
she didn't think she could beat it.
Luckily, she had some help!

When you're a monster,
it's good to have monster friends.
There is Dr. Cockroach, PhD,

and B.O.B.,

and The Missing Link,

and Insectosaurus.

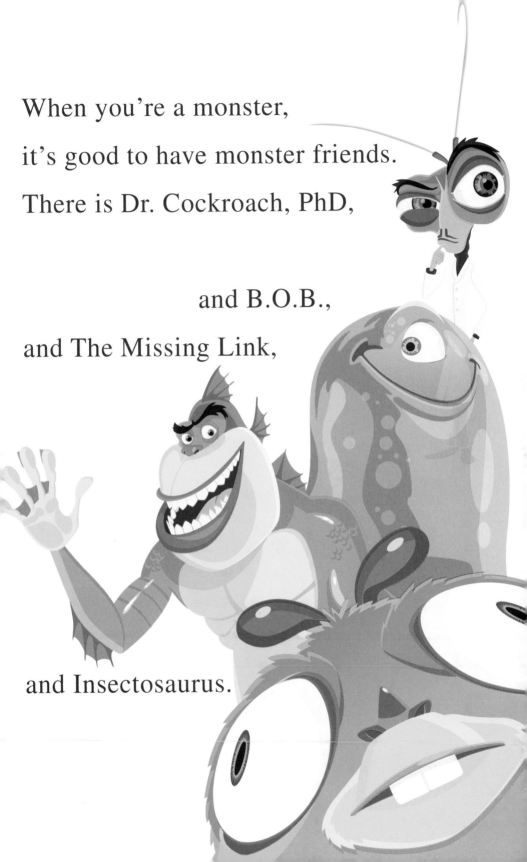

The giant robot chased Ginormica.
Ginormica felt like an ordinary girl.
Ordinary girls do not fight robots.
But she knew she had to try.
Ginormica battled the robot
on a big bridge.

Crash! The robot fell down.

"I did it!" said Ginormica.

"The robot failed,"

Gallaxhar's computer told him.

"I'll get that human myself!"

Gallaxhar shouted.

Gallaxhar's ship sped through space.

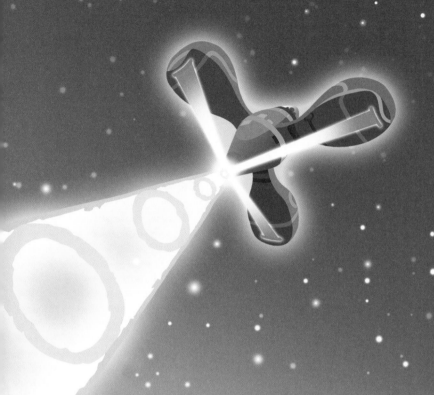

When Gallaxhar found Ginormica,

he beamed her up to his ship.

"I want the quantonium!"

Gallaxhar yelled at Ginormica.

He trapped her, then pulled a lever.

The quantonium left Ginormica's body.
It filled a ball on top of a statue.
Ginormica grew smaller and smaller.
She was back to being Susan Murphy,
small and ordinary.

Gallaxhar hooted with glee.

"When I was young,

everyone was mean to me," he said.

"But it won't happen anymore.

Now everyone will be just like me!"

Gallaxhar stepped into a machine.

The quantonium glowed.

Stamp! Out came a copy of Gallaxhar,
then another and another.

Hundreds of Gallaxhars came to life.

They were clones of the evil alien.

They were ready to take over Earth!

"Take away the human prisoner!"
Gallaxhar ordered some clones.

But the clones were really

Susan's monster friends in disguise.

They had snuck on board to save her!

The monsters led Susan away.

"Quickly!" said Dr. Cockroach.

"We must destroy Gallaxhar's clones."

"You go on without me," Susan said.

"I can't help.

I'm not Ginormica anymore."

The monsters didn't want to,

but they had to leave Susan.

"To the computer!"

said Dr. Cockroach.

"I'll shut down the cloning machine!"

Dr. Cockroach got to the computer.

He got to work on the wires.

But clones were coming at them!

Gulp! B.O.B. swallowed some clones.

The Missing Link fought off the others.

There were more clones.

And they found Susan!

Susan dodged this way and that.

"Wow!" Susan said to herself.
"Small, ordinary Susan Murphy
is getting away."
Maybe she could defeat Gallaxhar
after all!

Just then the computer said,

"The clone machine is shut down.

The clone army is defeated."

"Close all doors!" yelled Gallaxhar.

Gallaxhar had trapped the monsters.

Only Susan was free.

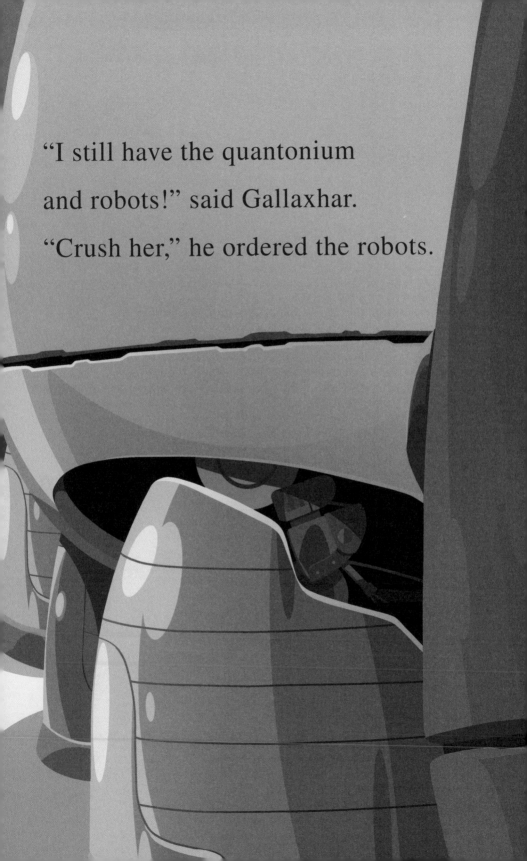

"I still have the quantonium
and robots!" said Gallaxhar.
"Crush her," he ordered the robots.

Susan knew she had to act quickly.

She zipped past robots and lasers.

Susan raced to Gallaxhar.

She raised her arm to strike

and hit the statue!

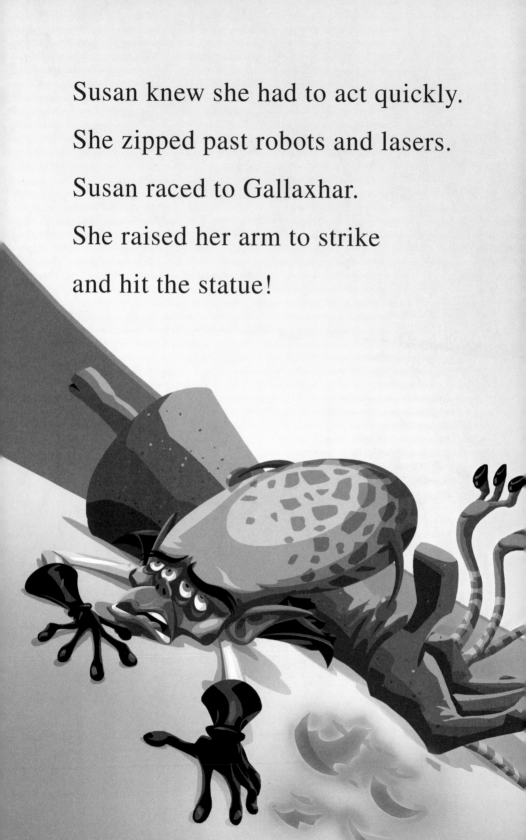

The statue fell on top of Gallaxhar.

He was trapped.

The quantonium ball shattered.

The quantonium spilled all over Susan.

Ginormica was back!

All the lasers and fighting

had wrecked the ship.

Crack! The ship was breaking apart!

"This ship will explode in two minutes,"

said the computer.

"Oh, no!" Ginormica said.
She punched through a door
and rescued her friends.
She held the monsters tight.
Down they fell
as the walls began to buckle.

"Five seconds to destruction,"
the computer's voice rang out.
"Four, three, two . . ."
Then Susan saw something amazing.
Insectosaurus had turned into
a butterfly and had come to help.

Everyone climbed onto Insectosaurus.

Away the monsters flew,

just as the computer said, "Zero!"

Boom! The ship exploded.

The aliens had lost!

The monsters had won!

Now Susan knew she was not ordinary.

No matter her size,

she would always be Ginormica!